D1636166

The Destroyer

THE DAY REMO DIED

Warren Murphy and Richard Sapir

THE DESTROYER #0: THE DAY REMO DIED

Originally published in The Assassin's Handbook (first published by Pinnacle Books, © 1982)

Published in 2015 by Destroyer Books/Warren Murphy Media

Requests for reproduction or interviews should be directed to DestroyerBooks@gmail.com

Front cover art by Gere Donovan Press

ISBN-13: 9781944073992
ISBN-10: 194407399X

A Note from Warren Murphy

Dick Sapir and I started writing an adventure novel in 1962. We thought we had a pretty good main character, a pretty good story and we even had a big-deal secret: **karate**, which hardly anyone in America had ever heard of at that time. We even threw in a pretty formulaic martial arts teacher named Chiun. And presto-changeo, there was "Created the Destroyer," the first book in the series—now at 150 books and counting.

Overnight successes we weren't. It took us eight years to finally get the book published. And while we felt it was pretty good, better than most of the stuff out there, we also knew the times they were a-changing. For better or for worse, ours was a pretty routine adventure and we knew routine adventure wasn't going to hack it, not in this rapidly-changing world.

So we wound up pushing our Destroyer series in the direction of mysticism and mythology and along the way, Chiun, our one-time ordinary karate teacher, became not just larger than life but bigger, bolder and greater than life itself, and the whole myth of The House of Sinanju and the magic relationship between Remo Williams and Chiun was born.

But making magic takes time. It took us many books and a lot of trial and error before we figured out exactly what the series was, what it wasn't, and what it could be. We knew we had it nailed, though, when Dick and I took another look at the Destroyer's beginnings, this time through our new and higher-focus lens, in a story called "The Day Remo Died." This story isn't an "alternate beginning"—the events that take place are the same as "Created"—but it's far more than just a companion piece. It's a look at the first book through the eyes of Sinanju, and a great place to begin (or resume!) reading the series. We had fun writing it, and, all these years later, it's still a fun read. I hope you enjoy it, too.

— WBM

CHAPTER ONE

HIS NAME WAS CHIUN and he was the Master of Sinanju and he was alone.

None came to the village on the West Korea Bay anymore. No emissaries from emperor or king. The pharaohs were dead. Persia was no more.

All those who had come to the House of Sinanju were no more.

Nor was there tribute anymore. No coins of gold or caravans of silk for a Master of Sinanju.

And soon that would not matter anymore because there would be no Master of Sinanju to receive them. The young were not interested anymore, and those who were could not learn the discipline that had made Sinanju famous throughout the royal courts of the world.

If the young men were not running off to Pyongyang, the capital of what was now the northern part of Korea, they were enlisting in the army to fight with guns and learn those lesser, easier ways.

It was not that they lacked courage. Courage was something that did not matter. It was just another emotion if one understood what the discipline of the House of Sinanju was about. Fear was no different from happiness.

What the young men lacked, for the first time in more than four thousand years, was that essence of a master. Somehow they could not grasp it. They thought a blow was something that was struck and not created. They thought speed came from the muscles as some form of quickness a person could control.

And they could not hear what Chiun was saying. It was as if there was no one with the Sinanju ear, to hear what this Master had learned from the previous Master, who had learned it from all of them who had gone before.

It was not there in the young.

And so Chiun sat in the darkness alone. He did not need the light that other men needed. He sat in the frigid sub-zero cold in a light kimono because he did not need the warmth of heavy clothing and furs. His body knew how to create warmth; his eyes knew how to see what had to be seen.

Scientists would have said that he and all the Masters of Sinanju had learned to harness the full human body. But the old Master would only think of it as "the knowing"—not unleashing primitive forces of the animal man, but being one with what he should be. For that was Sinanju. What a person should be.

And when Chiun died alone, it would be no more. It could not be written because reading it would only be hearing words. It had to be told from one to another, from one who knew to one who could someday know.

But even if there were another, the emperors and pharaohs and kings of greatness were gone. None had come to the House of Sinanju since the last war. When the world was filled with soldiers, who needed the skill of an assassin? And then, at a great distance, the Master heard something.

A young boy—one, too, who had failed to learn the discipline of Sinanju—came running up the single frozen-mud street of the village to the great house with the rare woods in which sat Chiun, doomed to be the last Master of Sinanju.

The boy wore a thick padded jacket and heavy leather

shoes, as if he were as frail as a white man.

"O, Master, O, Master," he cried. "There is a submarine in the bay, and the People's Army will not fire because it comes to honor you. And even the People's Army fears and respects the Master of Sinanju."

"Gracious Master," said Chiun.

"I mean gracious Master, O Master."

He could have told the boy that the army did not fear him, for armies feared no one. Armies had no minds. They did what they were told, and if their weak training gave way, they collapsed. Armies did not have minds and never had. The leaders alone had minds. And the leader in Pyongyang knew that there was no wall thick enough nor guard canny enough to stop a Master of Sinanju. So in all North Korea this village alone was spared from the rule of Kim Il Sung's army. For the maximum leader of Korea for life had a throat and so did his son. And he knew about the Master of Sinanju.

Chiun did not tell the boy about armies, for he was not worthy to know it. Instead he gave the boy a gold coin for the information. He did not tell the boy that the coin was worth more than its gold because it was a perfect likeness of Tiberius Caesar, as freshly minted as the day Tiberius himself had presented one hundred of them to the House of Sinanju as

4

tribute for its services. The boy knew only that it was gold. There were so many things he did not know and would never know, so many things that would pass from the earth because the House of Sinanju could not find from the village it had so long supported one young man to learn the discipline.

So the boy went, never to know the treasure he held, and the submarine sent a boat to shore, and a white man came. He walked up through the village to the house of the many different woods, the house where Chiun lived.

The white man came to the door and, looking inside, saw nothing, because for him it was dark.

"Hello," he said in a language that was English.

And the white man waited. On his left arm was a hook where a hand had been. He was breathing heavily, his body laden with the bulk of animal fats, and he breathed from his very pores the essence of alcohol, that lingering sweetness the body gave off, mixed with the rancidness of the fat he had eaten just that morning. The alcohol was at least four days old.

"Hello. I am looking for the Master of Sinanju. Are you there? Do you exist?"

"Who are you?" said Chiun.

"My name is Conn MacCleary, and I come with greetings from America and wish to pay tribute."

"America?"

"Yeah. You know, the country that fought North Korea down south of here. The one that sent you tribute and promised not to send one tank near the village of Sinanju when we crossed north of the Thirty-eighth Parallel."

"Oh, that one."

"I brought the tribute from General MacArthur to you."

"Oh, yes."

"But you weren't in. And I just left the gold here at the steps and was hoping you got it. Did you get it?"

"Your General MacArthur lived?"

"Of course."

"So why then would you ask if the gold was received? It was received."

"I bring more gold."

"I have no need of gold," Chiun said.

"Isn't it traditional that the House of Sinanju takes gold in tribute to support its villagers?"

"Yes."

"But you do not want this gold?"

"You may leave it," Chiun said.

"We seek your services."

"Ah. You wish a Master of Sinanju to secure a throne. Did

6

your General MacArthur become king as he hoped to?"

"No, no. He retired."

"What is retired?"

"He stopped working as a general, as a conqueror. He was told to stop."

"You put him in chains then," Chiun said. "The king realized what he was up to."

"No, no. We don't have a king," MacCleary said.

"Then why do you come here?"

"We want you to train someone. May I come in?"

"Yes."

"It's cold in here. Do you have a light?"

"I have enough light," said Chiun. "It is you who needs a light."

"Yes, I do. May I have one?"

"What is this? You come into my house and you ask for heat. Then you ask for light. And you say you are come with tribute? You have come with demands. I am not your servant. You have a coat; that is your heat. If you have a lantern, that is your light."

"Okay. I didn't know I was asking too much for a light."

"If you want light, wait until morning," Chiun said.

"I'm sorry," said the American, setting down a battery-powered flashlight. He clicked it and could not contain a gasp. The Master of Sinanju was old. The skin was wrinkled like a yellow raisin. Tufts of white hair hung in wisps around the ears. And in this nine-below-zero temperature, the old man was sitting in a thin black silk kimono.

"You're old," said the American.

"For an apricot, yes. For a head of lettuce, even more so. For a mountain, I am not even begun in years. However, for a man, I am just right, near the four score."

"I am sorry. I expected someone younger. The House of Sinanju is famed for the greatest assassins of all time, the sun source of all the martial arts, O Master."

"For a barbarian, you know a bit," Chiun said.

"I work for a secret organization in America."

"You are a religious cult," Chiun said.

"No, no. Our president—our elected king, if you will— fears that we cannot survive living with our Constitution unless we have a secret organization to make it work."

Chiun nodded. The man was off into unintelligible white drivel that made no sense to the intelligent mind. The president was not a king; the laws would not work; no one wanted to admit the laws did not work; therefore they had to have a secret organization to make sure the country did not descend into chaos. And to make the whole thing work, they needed one assassin. But it could not be a foreigner; it had to be an American citizen. And there could only be one, so that the government would not risk exposure, because as Chiun, the great Master of Sinanju himself knew, five people could not keep a secret. Therefore one assassin. And Chiun would train him, if he would. So babbled on the white man.

"Would you care for some tea?" asked Chiun.

"Does that mean you say yes?"

"No, no. You need tea, because if you don't have it, you will pass out from the cold, and I will have to get rid of your body."

"What do you think of my proposition?"

"We wish," Chiun said, "a long and happy reign to your king and may his enemies die of plague."

"Why the plague, O Master?" said the American.

"Because the hand of Sinanju will not be raised against them."

"You're saying no."

"You dribble on for almost an hour about people who do not exist and laws that do not work but you want to keep them anyway, and then you ask me if a no is a no. Yes. A no is a no. No."

"We will pay much gold, more gold than a pharaoh."

"I do not need gold."

"What do you need?"

"I need for prophecies to be more than half true," said Chiun. It did not matter that he told this to a stranger. Nothing mattered now. It had been prophesied long before that just before the end of the second millennium of the western calendar, Sinanju would not find its new Master in a living Sinanju villager. Part of that was true. It had not found a villager. It had found no one.

"What prophecy?" asked the white.

"It does not concern you. Let me make you your tea because it is easier to make tea than to haul a body."

And so the Master of Sinanju, like a woman in the village, brewed a cup of hot tea and gave it to the white man.

While he drank, the white talked. "It doesn't matter. It probably wouldn't have worked anyhow. I was making it simpler for you. You know, if you had said yes, we were going to have to arrange an execution and kill your pupil first, before you ever got to him."

"A non-living pupil?" Chiun asked.

"Yes, in a way. Yes. He is going to be officially dead. Fingerprints removed from files and everything. The perfect

10

man for an organization that does not exist. A man who doesn't exist. A dead man."

"Another cup of tea?" Chiun said.

"Why?"

"Because one will only get you down the road, and a second will get you to your boat, and I am going with you."

"You changed your mind?"

"I never change my mind. You changed the facts."

There was talk of gold payment, but Chiun had only one primary demand; that the student be his and no one else's. The white agreed to this, but the student would work for the organization called CURE. Chiun said he would not interfere with employment, as long as the student wished to serve CURE.

"Tell me more about this man," said Chiun, helping the bulky one to the door.

He was, said the man, a perfect specimen, the best that CURE could find.

"Wonderful, wonderful," said Chiun. "And he is, of course, a Leo."

"I don't know. I don't know what his horoscope is."

"I thought you said you knew everything about him."

"We didn't think a horoscope was that important."

"How typically white," said the Master of Sinanju.

It was announced to the village that the Master was leaving, and the proper ceremonies were performed, including tributes and laudations. Chiun noted every man in the village, all who had tried and failed. It was sad that none was born with the essence. But a greater sadness had been averted. There would be new blood to the House of Sinanju, according to the prophecy. During the ceremony, someone mentioned that the American had passed out from the cold while waiting in the boat for Chiun.

Chiun said that was all right, because the man with the hook had already made it to the boat, so there would not have to be any lugging of his body.

CHAPTER TWO

DR. HAROLD W. SMITH watched the ambulance pull into Folcroft Sanitarium with the last piece that made CURE.

Hours before, the state of New Jersey, in its last execution, had electrocuted a Newark policeman who, until the end, proclaimed his innocence.

Smith knew the policeman was innocent, because Smith had framed him. As had Conn MacCleary, back from the Orient with that peculiar old man.

MacCleary had worked in Asia and had assured Smith that this Master of Sinanju was the only one who could train the one assassin that CURE needed to survive.

"They got legends about these guys, Smitty. They go up and down walls, even through walls. Everything that has ever come out of the martial arts—even the night killers of Ninja—they come from what others figured out about Sinanju centuries back."

"I am aware of references to the House of Sinanju throughout history," Smith had said. "What I want to know is how accurate they are."

"We're going to find out," MacCleary said.

"Wonderful," Smith had said in a bitter tone. By nature and design of his genes, he had a lemony face, a perfect reflection of his spirit. He had been chosen to establish and run CURE because he was incorruptible, and also precise and unromantic. He would not lead this secret organization into excesses. Moreover, he could be trusted to dismantle it should it ever be in danger of being exposed.

The one thing Smith hated was surprise—finding out if something worked only when one had to try it as a last resort.

But in this matter there was no other choice. All the known training of the western world would not suffice to train just one assassin to do the work of many.

And then the Master of Sinanju had arrived in Folcroft with MacCleary, trailing fourteen giant ornate steamer trunks, wearing robes that would attract attention during an earthquake, and harboring a single disheartening superstitious question.

"What is his birth sign?"

"What?" Smith had said, stiffening in his gray three-piece suit.

"Is he a Leo?" asked Chiun, wearing his golden greeting robes.

"That's a star sign, isn't it?"

"Yes. Leos are the best assassins because they are more noble, more gracious and, of course, more effective."

"I don't know."

And then the Oriental who did not wish to know the personality profile of the man he would be training, nor the flexation factors of the muscles, asked only the birthdate of Remo Williams. From memory, Smith told the old man the date that the newborn orphan had been left on the steps of the Newark orphanage.

"A Virgo," Chiun said. "That is all right. There have been Virgos who have been fine. But, of course, the best is Leo. The Great Wang must have been a Leo. And I, of course, I am a Leo."

"I see. Well, you will be able to begin your training in a week. He should be recovered then from the drugs which made him appear dead at the execution."

"Appear dead?" said Chiun.

15

"Yes. We short-circuited this execution device so that our man would not really die. But for all records and practical purposes, he is a dead man. You see?"

Smith saw outrage on the old, weathered face.

"You may be wondering," Smith said, "whether he has been informed of this frame-up. He hasn't yet. But the psychological profile says he will serve once he learns what happened to him."

"He will not die?" said Chiun.

"Of course not," Smith said.

"Then there is no reason for me to stay." And the old Oriental had risen, turned, and left the room. MacCleary reported minutes later that Chiun was packing all fourteen steamer trunks.

"We've got to have him," Smith said. "Peculiar or not, he can't leave."

"How do we stop him?" MacCleary asked. "From what I hear, we couldn't even hit him with a bullet."

"He says he won't train this Williams because Williams isn't really dead. That doesn't make any sense. What's going on?" Smith asked.

MacCleary shrugged.

"You're the expert," Smith snapped. "You're supposed to

16

know."

"All I know is that he wasn't that interested in anything I had to offer until I mentioned that Remo was going to be dead. Then he wanted to train him. I think we lucked out by accidentally walking into one of their legends."

"So much for lucking out because the luck has turned. Don't let him leave. Offer him something else."

MacCleary was back in less than half an hour.

"He doesn't want anything else, Smitty. He wants only a dead man."

"Did you ever promise him a dead man?"

"No, not that I remember. I said we were going to have an execution. I guess the old guy heard what he wanted to hear."

"Then he is breaking his contract," Smith said.

"I don't think they go by contracts," MacCleary said.

"I think you're wrong," said Smith with steady logic. "I think that would be the one thing a house of assassins would have to honor if they were going to last century after century. I think if anything is going to work, that will."

"I'll do it. But I don't think it will matter to him. I think he is the last assassin of the House of Sinanju."

"Then maybe it will matter more. Ask him if he wants to be the first Master of Sinanju to break a…call it, a solemn holy contract. Yes," said Smith. "A solemn holy contract."

MacCleary was back shortly, flushed with success. "Chiun, the last Master of Sinanju, agrees to train Remo Williams until his first service."

"What does that mean?"

"He didn't say," MacCleary had said, and that had solved the crisis. But even as the word from the Folcroft infirmary came that the patient had arrived, Smith wondered what the next crisis would be and if, after all, they had not made a mistake.

• • •

It was time to see their new recruit.

Smith met Chiun in the hall outside the infirmary. Chiun was aloof. Smith said hello, and Chiun allowed a cold, precise minuscule nod.

"I was wondering what first service meant. What you meant by his 'first service'?"

"I live by my contracts," Chiun said. "If one holds another to a contract, one should at least know what that contract is."

"Why are you so bothered by the fact that your pupil won't be dead?" Smith asked.

"I am not bothered. You should be bothered. It is you who broke the promise. It is you who should worry," Chiun said.

18

"May I ask you? How would you expect to train someone who was truly dead?"

"First, according to what will be, as was said long ago. I shall not find within the village he who can learn Sinanju. Secondly, I will train one not from the living. Therefore dead."

"And I ask you again, Master of Sinanju," said Smith. "How is it that a man can die and still be trained?"

"Ordinarily I would not bother answering," said Chiun. "But you have contracted with the House of Sinanju, and you will receive service as other kings and emperors received service. So I will tell you. A finger dies and you still live even though it is cut off. An arm goes and you still live, even though it is cut off. Men have lived without limbs or eyes or ears, and still they live. So too can they live without the heart or the lungs or the brain. It is that which is underneath all things and beyond all things that makes a person a person."

"You mean the soul," Smith said.

"I mean what I mean," said the Master of Sinanju, and said no more but folded his bony hands into the kimono and walked down the hall with the emperor who had lied.

He would see his pupil and train him until first service. It would not, of course, be Sinanju. He would teach him to approach and strike and then, when first service was done,

19

Chiun would return to Sinanju and await the really-dead of the prophecy—if it should ever come to pass.

The white man stopped just outside the door. "He doesn't know where he is or what this is all about," said Smith. "We will have to explain it to him before you begin training."

"You mean he does not know he will be glorified by the rays of Sinanju?"

"He doesn't even know he is going to be working for us. But his psychological profile shows he will definitely serve. He is a variation of a compulsive obsessive with a basic chronic depressive goal-oriented mode."

"That is not common English you speak?" said Chiun.

"No, no. Translated, it means that once this man gets into it, he's into it. We have a patriot. In the best sense."

"So he is going to be your assassin, and he doesn't know yet?"

"No. Not yet."

"His spirit is not committed?" Chiun asked.

"How could it be? The last thing he remembers is passing out from the drugs that got him through the fake execution. You understand, of course, why we had to have someone entirely removed from the possibility of identification."

Chiun looked at the white man and nodded. Of course he did not understand. Only another lunatic would understand.

20

But he knew from earliest training how to treat an emperor, even if this lunatic refused to be called one.

"Of course, of course," Chiun said. "How could he? Does a rainbow know it is a rainbow? Or a star a star? How wise," said Chiun to the demented one.

"Yes. I think I understand your philosophy," said Smith.

In English, Chiun said, "All things are simple to your piercing mind, O Emperor." And in Korean, he mumbled, "Lunatic."

Chiun waited until Smith had cleared the doctors out of the room. When he finally went in, he did not even look at the person in the hospital bed, but began as every master had with every pupil, by looking at the feet.

The feet were very white, Chiun noticed, quite pale, almost as pale as Smith. Some Koreans were light. And Japanese—many of them were light. Of course, a Japanese would breed with anyone. And the Chinese would try to breed with anyone.

The man was obviously a meat-eater because his feet showed he failed to finish his full step, a common flaw of the West, which even some people of normal skin color had adopted during the invasion of western ideas.

One could also smell the meat emanating from its pores.

21

Yet, smell was not the main examining tool. The eyes were, and they had to go from foot to head.

The calves were overly muscled; the nervous system, almost unused but for minimal natural functions.

Thighs overly muscled and very pale.

So too with the stomach. Obviously this man had been infected with those ideas of western exercise where they thought muscles made strength. The Japanese, too, were like that.

Chiun allowed a moment of hope to the forces of the universe: Please. Do not let this too-pale student be a Japanese.

The burns on the wrists and ankles, according to the crazed white, Smith, were from electrodes in the imitation of an electrocution. The skin did burn well so that, despite the beef, there was good blood flow. If the nervous system were totally untrained, then, of course, the muscles had to carry everything.

The lungs were a disaster.

"What do you think?" said the white, Smith.

"I haven't finished."

"I was wondering what you were looking for," Smith said. "Our doctors have examined him thoroughly."

"Of course, of course, O Emperor Smith. The best doctors in the world, no doubt," Chiun said. He did not mention that they, too, probably did not care what his birth sign was, either, but just went right to the organs as white doctors always did in their cultural ignorance, as though illness was some strange, mysterious process that affected man and animals alike.

The neck, too, was overly muscled and the wrists too thin. The place that should have bulk had none. The wrists were as useless as the body of a harlot in a Bombay crib.

And the lips were pink, too. Too pink. Chiun then let himself see the eyes.

"Eeeeeeeahhhhh," he screamed, stepping back.

The eyes were round!

Round eyes!

"He's white," screamed Chiun.

"Of course," said the crazed Smith. "He must move unnoticed in our environment."

"He is totally white?"

"So far as we know. He's an orphan."

"Possibly he has a Korean grandparent, yes?"

"No, not likely," the crazed Smith said. "The records are sketchy, but I don't think any Korean."

"Perhaps eastern Russian. There is some good blood there."

"No. We don't think there's any Tatar blood."

"Genghis Khan was good people. For a horseman, that is.

The Mongol always loved his horse. Tamerlane was more citified, you know. But sweet Genghis was more like Attila. They always loved the horse. You can conquer from a horse, but you cannot rule from a horse."

"I am not intending to go on horseback, Master of Sinanju, and no, I am sorry, but Remo is one hundred percent white."

"You are sorry," said Chiun. "You? You do not have to train him. And how do you pronounce that name again?"

"Remo," said Smith.

"Where does the tongue go?" asked Chiun, watching Smith's lips. The thin white lips opened, and the tongue fell back, making that white sound.

Chiun shook his head. "Emperor, I will call him by a simpler name. I will call him Eeeooooaauiiii."

"May I advise against it? He will keep his first name forever. He will never give it up. It is something in his character."

"Ah, well," sighed Chiun. "How do you place the tongue again, O Gracious Emperor?"

"Remo," said Smith.

"Remo," said Chiun.

"Oooooh," said the man in the bed, coming back toward consciousness and hearing his name.

There were, of course, other problems to the training. Remo—all right, if that were his name, he would be called that—had a basic negative attitude and was under the impression, as were many whites, that white skin was best.

"Gook," was his word for the Master of Sinanju.

This was answered by a stroke of gentle persuasion, and after an hour of rolling around the floor moaning, he realized, this Remo thing, that "gook" was not the proper title for a Master of Sinanju.

The ignorance, though, became even worse. He thought the Master's beautiful Korean countenance was Chinese. For that, two hours of rolling on the floor.

All the white was concerned about was eating.

He had to be shown he had layers of fat yet to be used up. Why eat?

"I'm hungry," said the white thing.

"Yes?"

"Well, I want to eat."

"Of course. You haven't eaten for a day. You will always want to eat if you go twenty-four hours without food. But you don't need to eat. You already have fat deposits to live on."

"But I wanna eat," said Remo.

"So?"

"What do you mean, so? I got a right to eat. Hey, maybe you don't know it, but I don't want to be here."

"I didn't invite you here," the Master said.

"Yes. Well, I didn't invite myself. I was framed. Do you know that, goo…Chiun?"

"Gracious Master will do," said Chiun.

"You're not my Master. No one's my master," said Remo. His wrists still hurt from the chair. He wanted a good thick hamburger. He wanted a nice soft mattress. He wanted more than any of that to get out of this place with the crazy gook who was not to be called a Chinaman.

"Your stomach is your master," said Chiun. On the third day, because the student was at least trying and, for a white, doing adequately, Chiun prepared a delicacy with his own hands.

Immediate ingratitude was shown.

"What is this crapola?" asked Remo.

"That crapola, as you call it," said Chiun, letting the exact nature of the delicacy sink into the white mind, letting the white know what had been put before him in splendor, "that crapola, as you call it, is steamed seaweed and eel brains over week-old rice."

"Yeah, right. It tasted just like that."

"Then why did you make vomiting noises?" asked Chiun. Again he asked for a hamburger or a steak with tomato sauce and other abominations of the western stomach.

"I could give you that," said Chiun. "But I am bound here with you until you perform your first service. Why delay it? Do your training, then we both may leave."

"First service? Oh, you mean that killing stuff."

Chiun sat the crude white down.

"No, not killing stuff," he said. "You will attempt to become an assassin. An assassin does not do killing stuff. A truck can do killing stuff. Meat of cows, eaten regularly, does killing stuff. But a professional assassin promotes harmony in a regime, restores faith in monarchy, and brings about a more peaceful humor to the entire community."

"You're making a hit sound like a public service."

"Assassination, professional assassination, is the highest public service."

"It's a hit," said Remo.

"Spoken like someone who would call eel brains crapola."

"Right. Crapola."

"All right," the Master said. "If you must persist, then let us make a deal, Remo. Are you happy now that I use what passes for a name among you creatures?"

27

"It's my name," Remo said.

"I didn't give it to you."

"I don't know who gave it to me. I don't even know my parents."

"A pair of whites," said Chiun, clearing up the matter. "Pay attention. You didn't ask to be white, and so it is not your fault. You didn't ask to be here, either, and perhaps that is not your fault. I was deceived and you were deceived. So let us make this pact. I will train you to your first service, and then I will leave."

"Does that mean they'll let me out of here?"

"Absolutely. You must go out to do the service," Chiun said.

"Then I split."

"You do not hear me begging you to follow me. Just do the first service."

"It's a hit, you know," said Remo.

"If you wish to call it that."

"What do you call it?" Remo asked.

"It is a service," said Chiun.

"I think of it as killing."

"In your hands, it undoubtedly will be," said the Master of Sinanju.

28

He had little hope for this white man. But hardly had the breathing techniques begun, when he noticed something strange.

The white man could center the air right away. Almost all the boys from the village took months to center the air in their lungs, instead of just gulping. But this one imitated perfectly. Of course, it was an accident. A one-in-a-billion chance that by some freak of nature, he could do it well the first time.

"That's it? That's the big deal?" said Remo. "So what does this do?"

"If you don't breathe correctly, you don't move correctly."

And of course the white wanted to know what a move looked like. He was sitting on a wooden floor. Chiun severed a few wooden slats with his fingers, so that the white might observe how the muscles did not do the move, but were the move.

"Holy sheet. You cut a four-foot hole in the damned floor," said Remo.

"Breathing," explained Chiun.

Remo confided that he had been raised in an orphanage and never really had a home. It was a Catholic orphanage in Newark, closed now. He had been a Marine. He had played high school football. He really didn't have anyone in the world.

He had hoped to have a family and a house and children, and then he was framed for a murder and got sucked into this project that Chiun was in.

"Your problem is," Chiun said, "that you are selfish. You think only of yourself."

"Who should I think of?"

"You might think of me."

"Yeah? What's your problem?" Remo said.

"I don't discuss my problems. I don't mention ingratitude and crazed emperors."

"You've done nothing but talk of what an unworthy asshole Smith is since I met you and how you are stuck with an unworthy white. That's all I hear. White, white, white."

"I only mention a fraction of what I think."

"And from a gook…yeah, gook," said Remo, getting out of the sitting position that made his joints ache, and moving to his feet. "Go ahead. Kill me. Go ahead. You can kill me. If you think that makes you better, kill me."

"Of course it makes me better," Chiun said.

"Gook," said Remo, and with one fingerstroke Chiun put him into great pain, writhing on the floor. Such was Remo's agony that tears flowed while he did not cry. The back arched, and only the head and feet touched the ground, and when the

30

last desperate bit of breath came back to him, the one word he said was, "Gook."

And Chiun took him out of his pain. This white did not break. It was said in Sinanju that the best Masters were often the most difficult to subdue in training. Of course, this Remo thing was not being trained in full Sinanju.

And it came to pass that the meat smell left the white as his diet improved, and the breathing brought about balance, and he was taken to walls to learn how to climb.

And he kept falling.

Chiun said, "You fall because you are afraid. Fear is nothing more than a feeling. You feel hot. You feel hungry. You feel angry. You feel afraid. Fear can never kill you. So what are you afraid of?"

"It sounds crazy, Chiun, but I am afraid of being afraid."

"Ahh," said Chiun. "The greatest fear. You are quite perceptive for a white man."

"Will you stop with that white stuff already?"

"I said nothing. The problem with you whites is that you are overly sensitive."

Through the months, the body fat went. The wrists thickened, properly, as if the genes for thick wrists were always there but had been dormant. The breathing got better and better. There were even times when Chiun had wished this were a Sinanju youngster and, one time, while working against the presence of a wall to teach elevation, he whispered the word "Perfect." It was said in Korean, of course, and of course Remo did not understand it.

He had started to pick up a few words of Korean here and there. But it was the little obscenities he seemed to remember best.

"I don't know where you get that kind of language," said Chiun.

One day, when the good breathing finally controlled the other movements, Chiun brought Remo to a small stand of birch in the courtyard of Folcroft.

It was spring, and Chiun was careful to make sure that Remo felt no violence in him. Even in Oriental teachings, the stroke always had much violence allowed to it, and that violence reflected hate, which was a form of fear. And fear limited the power so that only the muscles could be used and not the mind.

And so as they passed the stand of birch, Chiun told Remo to put his hand through the trunk of one of the trees, to reach a butterfly on the other side.

"Touch it gently," said Chiun.

And Remo's hand was going out before he knew what he was doing. He only understood as the hand came back.

"Holy yak dung," gasped Remo in Korean. The birch had splintered in the middle where his hand had met it.

The upper branches creaked as the tree bent to close down the white pulpy gash that had been exploded out. The tree was held by only half a trunk.

"How'd you do that?" said Remo.

"I didn't," Chiun said.

"Well, I sure as hell didn't."

"Yes, you did."

"I didn't do anything," said Remo. He felt his hand. It tingled a bit, but it couldn't have gone through a thick birch trunk.

He looked at his fingernails.

"Not even a splinter."

"If there had been a splinter, you wouldn't have had a hand left," Chiun said.

"But I didn't even see my hand move."

"You will. You haven't worked on your sight yet." Chiun paused, then said, "Here. Quickly. Catch my hand on the other side." And Remo let his hand go out, and the birch groaned, and dropped and banged down into the courtyard.

33

A man with a lemon face and a gray suit came running out of one of the doors overlooking the courtyard. This was Smith, who supposedly ran everything. He lectured Chiun on showing things where others might see. He also mentioned how expensive trees were.

"Couldn't you use something other than a live tree for training?"

"Yes, most certainly," Chiun said. "There is something even better."

"Well, then. Tell us what it is, and we'll get it for you."

"Yak skulls," said Chiun. "A herd of yak would be perfect."

"Yes. Well," said Smith, clearing his throat. "Stay with the trees if you must, but please stay away from the birch. Try the maples."

"As you will, O Emperor," said Chiun. But even as he bowed, he could not help but approve of the way the birch had been severed. If only Remo were Korean. If only.

The next day, Smith asked how training was going. He had a problem, which might turn out well for the Master of Sinanju. Remo was about to do his first service.

CHAPTER THREE

TRAINING, SAID CHIUN TO SMITH, was going beautifully. They were in Smith's office, which overlooked Long Island Sound. It had those funny windows that could only be looked out from. Smith indeed was a peculiar emperor because he hid his power, when everyone knew that power that was not shown would eventually have to be used.

And, as the best assassins understood, the first use of power was to have your enemy respect your strength. Then the power would not have to be used at all.

"How soon can you have him ready?" Smith asked.

"Far ahead of schedule," said Chiun.

"Which is what, in terms of days?"

"Which is nothing in terms of days, O Emperor. In terms

of years. He has almost three tens of years now, which is late for an assassin to begin. But he is a very fast learner. And for a white, an incredibly fast learner. I would send him out on his forty-fifth birthday with, of course, a very simple service."

"What about Friday?" Smith said.

"That is only three days away."

"We're desperate. We were so desperate, we had to send MacCleary out on a mission. Now he is in great pain in a hospital, and we are afraid he will talk," Smith said.

"Talk?"

"Yes. Tell the world about us. He has been, in effect, captured."

"Then he should talk greatly," Chiun said. "Tell his captors of the vengeance of your power. Threaten death greatly."

"That's not what I want," Smith said.

"Of course not. It is too late for that," said Chiun. "Hang their heads out on Folcroft wall as warning to others."

"No, I don't want that, either. Remo has to go out and make sure MacCleary won't talk. One way or another. Do you understand?"

"He can't go," Chiun said.

"He goes, and thank you for your services. I guess this

qualifies as Remo's first service. We consider your contract fulfilled."

"It isn't fulfilled. He isn't ready," Chiun said.

"This is a war, and ready or not, he goes," Smith said.

"I have put in months. What about my work?"

"I'm sorry," Smith said. "He goes."

Chiun was supposed to send Remo up to see Smith. But before he did so, he told the young white that he should refuse the mission.

"Refuse, hell. I'm leaving. I'm taking whatever they give me and going. They can't get me. I have no records, no prints on file. I am the freest man in America."

"What about my work? You can't do anything yet."

"I can get out of here," Remo said, "and that's all I want to do."

"I have given you some karate tricks. Children's games," Chiun said. "You are still hopeless."

"Probably," Remo agreed. "I hate to say it, Chiun. But even though I hated everything at the beginning, I've kind of…well, I don't know. I can't find a word for it. It's sort of liking something but, it's not exactly that, either. You know what I mean?"

"Of course I know. I am the Master of Sinanju."

"It's like hearing with your entire body."

"Yes, that is what it is. You are exceptional. For a white."

"White, white, white," Remo said. "There you go again. You're not bad. For just a Korean."

Chiun shrugged. "Never just a Korean. I am Chiun."

"And I am Remo. Good-bye."

"That's it? Good-bye?"

"What do you want?" Remo asked.

"An ode of gratitude to a teaching Master would be appropriate."

"Okay. How do I do it?"

"It is an hour-long speech that begins with the laudations of 'Gracious Master, unto you we humbly glorify the House of which thy countenance…'"

"Screw that. Thanks," said Remo.

When Remo left his quarters, Chiun began to pack, each kimono correctly laid out and folded. Each sandal for the proper occasion.

He had intended only to teach a stroke or two, but he had actually given the beginnings of Sinanju because the young man was actually hearing with his entire body.

Things that even Korean lads struggled with, this white man had flowed into—while, of course, not knowing it.

It might be interesting, Chiun thought, to see what would happen to one so raw and so white on a first service. Besides, there was the name of Sinanju to think about. How could Sinanju be associated with one so clumsy?

All right. Chiun would oversee the first mission. He would make sure Sinanju would not be embarrassed. He would make sure the white with the funny name would at least perform a proper service and not get himself killed too quickly.

It would not be hard. Even though the barbarians in the street stared at one who was properly dressed, the Master did not have to hide from them. He had only to hide from Remo.

Chiun watched and saw that Remo did not run away from Smith and from his service. He wandered around, almost got himself killed, went about the service in a rough, clumsy way. Yet, there was the foundation of grace.

It was not, of course, a traditional smooth assassination. Remo made wisecracks to the targets. For some reason, he felt compelled to fornicate, although what he would do with the baby, Chiun could not fathom. At the end, he returned to Folcroft Sanitarium for further training, saying he had seen the light. He knew now what he would do with his life, he said.

"You see, I'm in this thing. I never had a home or a family, and I believe in this country. I believe in America. I believe it's worth a life."

At first, Chiun thought this manner of thinking was some form of temporary insanity that would soon pass. But the next day, too, Remo was talking like that. Right in the midst of his first try at an interior line attack upon single and multiple targets, he said it.

"I love America."

It was summer. And the grass on the Folcroft lawn was mellow and warm. Heat was about them, and Remo wore shorts while Chiun wore the red summer robe.

"You love what?" Chiun asked, letting the robe flutter.

"America," said Remo.

"I thought you said that. What is it you love about America?"

"Don't you love Korea?" Remo asked.

"No."

"You're always saying Koreans are better than everyone else."

"That is a fact of nature like gravity. I am Korean. That is enough for any people, even one that does not suffer the flaws of others."

40

"You don't love the Korean people?" Remo asked.

"Of course not."

"What do you believe in?"

"I don't believe in anything," Chiun said. "I know things."

"Well, I believe in something. I believe this country has given so many people so many chances that it deserves being defended and saved."

"Why?" asked the Master.

"Because I'm an American," said Remo.

So Smith was right. This man who had been framed by his government, scared out of his very being because he had thought he might really die, this white had nevertheless felt obliged to kiss the teeth that bit him.

Whites were often very tribal, Chiun realized. Remo did not own the country, owed it nothing, yet was willing to die for it. Which of course was the one thing an effective assassin was not supposed to do; only lunatics killed themselves.

"Assassins kill others," said Chiun. "That is basic. You do not get killed. You kill. Otherwise, it will be a very ineffective and short career you will have for yourself."

Remo asked him again if he believed in anything. Chiun had to believe in something, Remo said.

"I know who I am," Chiun said. "The Masters of Sinanju

41

all knew who they were. To know is not to have to believe. It is to know."

"I don't understand."

"You don't understand? You don't understand? You love this thing called a country, which you don't own, which has never done anything for you, and you say you don't understand someone who knows who he is? The insanity you feel is what armies are made of. I am trying to undo all the bad habits instilled in you by the American Army."

"Marines," said Remo.

"A different button, the same machine," said Chiun. "I cannot wait until you are sufficient not to embarrass the House of Sinanju. For at that moment, I leave. Gladly."

"It must be pretty close. Because I can do things now that I couldn't even imagine before."

"Because a bug is faster than a flower doesn't make it a bolt of lightning," Chiun said.

"Now, that nonsense I understand," Remo said.

"Yes. in Sinanju we tell it to three-year-olds."

"What do you tell people who are thirty?"

"Respect those who should be respected," Chiun said.

"I respect you. You don't think I respect you?"

"When have you ever given me a laudation? Where are

42

the recitations of 'O Gracious Master, thy bounteous beneficence doth radiate upon us lowly ones'? Where is it?"

"I don't go for that stuff," said Remo. "I figure that when I do something right, that's the greatest compliment you can get."

And the Master of Sinanju was silent. He left the training room for his own quarters that day, shocked by what he had heard. Because out of the mouth of this white man had come the very saying every new Master of Sinanju told the one who had trained him. It was that the normal laudations for the training Master were no longer appropriate because the very life of the new Master was the greatest laudation possible. That performance at the level of Sinanju was the greatest honor any Master could give to the one who went before.

Chiun had said this to his father, and his father to Hwa, and Hwa had said this to Koo, and Koo had said this to Sun, and Sun had said this to Myung. Wang the Great had said this, as well as the lesser Masters. All had said this, and now these words had come in the strange tongue of the white who could scarcely make the initial moves.

How could Remo have known such a thing? Granted, he had picked up the curse words from those occasional rare lapses that anyone teaching a white would make. But where

43

did he get the concept of the great laudation by the living of his life? Chiun had never mentioned that. But Remo had understood it.

Chiun thought about this for many days and then went to the office of Emperor Smith.

"O, Emperor, while I glorify your great name, I believe that perhaps one of your servants made a mistake."

"What are you getting at, Master of Sinanju?" Smith asked.

"Perhaps, in tracing the ancestry of your white assassin, they overlooked a person of true Korean heritage?"

"No," said Smith.

"Are you sure?" Chiun asked.

"Yes. When he was left at the orphanage, there were…well, definite indications that he had been born only shortly before. We were able to find out the hospital. But there were no babies born there to Korean parents about that time. Why do you ask?"

"No reason," said Chiun. "Then I must get ready to leave. I should stay no more. Remo is adequate for a white."

"I must say you have done an excellent job. If you wish to stay, we would appreciate continuing your services. The gold, of course, is being shipped regularly to your village by submarine."

44

"Yes, of course. The tribute."

"We could increase the tribute," Smith said.

What could Chiun answer? That the only reason he had asked for tribute was because, for four thousand years, all Masters of Sinanju had asked for tribute, that it was tradition. He did not need more gold to sit there in the house of rare woods on the West Korea Bay. Who would spend it? The village that the assassin's skill had always supported? The village that could no longer provide a successor to carry on the powers and knowledge of Sinanju? More gold for what?

And so Chiun only answered, "I have fulfilled my agreement. I must leave soon."

Already he had taught too much to one who would never carry on Sinanju. It was not Remo's fault that he was white. It was not his fault that he had not really died, according to the prophecy.

He had done extraordinarily well, considering. And in truth he had never given anything less than what was in him. And Chiun found himself wishing Remo had been born in the village of Sinanju or that one of the village boys had shown half the interest and talent as this poor white. Then Chiun himself would not have been here looking to fulfill a vague prophecy badly recorded on one of the oldest of the scrolls.

So he had to say good-bye, and that was it. He put Remo through the crude fragments of the basics of Sinanju one more time. It would keep him alive for a while. He could not, of course, expect to have a long life like a true Master of Sinanju, because he would be relying too much on brash courage and not on technique. He would have power here and there, and perhaps make several missions successfully, and then, because he was not complete, his mind would wander or his concentration would break, and he would be hit by a bullet or fall and be unable to recenter himself for landing and he would, like all other common assassins, die.

It was not Chiun's fault. He had already given him more than he should have. The white was not supposed to be Sinanju.

"Remo," he said in last advice.

"Yeah," said Remo. He was looking out the window, his eyes wandering. Here Chiun was, sad for leaving, a Master of Sinanju feeling sad for leaving, and this white thing was finding something more interesting to concentrate on. Like the sky outside.

"You were never a good student, and I wasted all my best teaching on a vessel unworthy," Chiun said.

"You always say that. What's so special about today?"

"I am leaving."

46

"Yeah? Why?"

"Because you're inadequate. You were always inadequate. That is why I am leaving."

"Okay," said Remo.

"Is that it? Okay?"

"Sure."

Chiun scrutinized the white face. The deep, dark eyes were open, the lips were calm, the face was at peace. He was not lying. He was not bothered.

"I am leaving and just 'okay'?"

"Well, I kind of liked you."

"Kind of liked a Master of Sinanju?" Chiun said.

"Yeah. I don't have anyone else. I had a dog once. He got heart worm. You know, Newark is near swamps, and there are mosquitoes."

"A dog," Chiun said.

"My dog. I loved that dog," Remo said.

"You loved a dog, and you kind of liked the Master of Sinanju?" Chiun said.

"Smitty did that psychological crapola on me. I've got problems with long-term personal relationships," Remo said. "Anyway, now I have Sinanju, so it doesn't really matter that you're going."

47

"You have but a single broken ray. You do not have Sinanju," Chiun said.

"You'd be amazed at how I took out guys."

"I saw," Chiun said.

"I didn't see you watching."

"Because you are not Sinanju," Chiun said.

"I don't believe you," Remo said.

As soon as the words were spoken, Chiun had Remo on the floor in pain.

"I'm still Sinanju," groaned Remo. "You're just better now." Chiun increased the pain, yet the stubbornness in this white did not let go. And he increased the pain again, and still the white acted as stubborn as always.

Pain would not do. There had to be something else. Chiun would teach him one more lesson, one last lesson before he left, so that Remo would not tell the world he was Sinanju and die doing so, disgracing both the House of Sinanju and the last Master of Sinanju, Chiun himself.

For relieving Remo of the pain, the following thanks were received by the Master of Sinanju.

"You're a real shit," said Remo.

"You're welcome," said Chiun.

CHAPTER FOUR

ABSELMO "BIG BUNS" BONAFANTE proudly examined his new handmade rosewood desk. It had been given him in a trade with the craftsman. For this handmade desk, Big Buns would let the craftsman keep his hands. Otherwise, Big Buns would have had them broken in many places.

Big Buns did not want to do this, but the craftsman had borrowed and failed to repay.

While tightening the wood vise on the craftsman's hands, Big Buns had told the screaming workman that he was really protecting the "free enterprise" system.

"What would happen if everybody borrowed and nobody paid back? The nation would be ruined."

"But I only borrowed a hundred dollars, and now I owe you three thousand," the craftsman cried.

"Interest," said Big Buns. "You got twenty-nine hundred in interest."

And then Big Buns said the big word he liked so much. The word he got from newspapers. The word he saw in bank windows. The word that had made America great.

"Compounded," said Big Buns. And then, of course, he had added his own brilliant little variation, his very own improvement on American banking practice. "Every minute. Compounded minute-ly."

He had gone up to Vermont for a vacation, lent the money, and at the end of the weekend came to collect. Failing that, he told the craftsman he would take something of comparable value.

It was the desk and he was proud of it.

But that morning, some of his business associates at his storefront in a Newark office said that he had been gypped.

"It's a wooden desk. Dat's all. Tree grand for a wooden desk. You been had, Big Buns."

Big Buns did not like hearing things like that, because Big Buns, although not to his face, had often been called unsuited for other areas of business. The other areas were anything that

50

required brains.

Big Buns was a head-breaker. When he wasn't breaking heads for men who made their living with their brains, he would collect debts or settle scores. Sometimes he would use a lead pipe, sometimes a gun; sometimes he would even use helpers. If any in that sort of business had understood the phrase, "idiot savant," they would have used it for Big Buns. Because while the man was certifiably moronic, he had an unequalled skill in harming and killing.

But like many true talents in a field, he wanted to branch out into others: extortion, blackmail, mail fraud, unions. All the ones that required brains.

So that when he collected a fine rosewood desk that indeed was worth every penny of the money he claimed was owed him, he felt angered that others, his colleagues, would think it just wood. Big Buns did not want to be thought of as stupid.

And they were, in a way, calling him stupid again.

"Whatcha gotta do, Big Buns, is get like a nice piece of formica, see, and you gotta screw it in real tight. And then you got something," said Salvatore "Toots" Tituccio. "It'll cover up all this wavy uneven stuff," he said, running his hand over the elegant rosewood grain, smoothed to a powder satin

51

finish by loving hands.

"You can put it in with brass tacks, see, if you really want something special," said the man who employed Big Buns for loan shark collection.

"I knew it would be a solid base for a good table," said Big Buns. "I wasn't figuring on using it raw." He scratched a match on the desktop to light his cigar.

The room had metal chairs with brown clothlike seats and tables that almost matched; see-through glass showing cheap chrome legs; a brownish wall case system that didn't even bother maintaining a pretense of wood; and lamps that looked as if they were won at a carnival. There were two such lamps, multicolored as if some cheap use had been found for a refuse clay bin.

It was the sort of furniture one did not repair or hand down, but discarded when used, like a breakfast food carton. The fine rosewood desk did not fit. Nor did the wood case of the intercom, which continued to buzz.

Big Buns, who had told his secretary he was in conference and not to be disturbed, was now being disturbed.

"Why you disturbing me?" he barked into the speaker.

The secretary's voice came back. "Mr. Bonafante, the gentleman refuses to leave."

"Does he know who I am?" asked Big Buns.

"He says he does and that is why he is here."

"Well, then, I will converse with him," said Big Buns, proud of the big word he had just used.

"Maybe you shouldn't," his secretary said.

"What harm can conversing do?" said Big Buns, proud of the variation of the word he had used. His hairy hands were broad as rib roasts and his body blended into a mountain of fleshy muscle. He had the kind of rough face that emptied restaurants. Now it was smiling because he had used the big word.

"He might say something that might offend you," the secretary said.

"Not to worry," said Big Buns with a benign smile.

"Tell the muscled baboon I want to use him," came another voice, squeaky and Oriental, over the speaker.

"Is that the faggot what said that?" Big Buns screamed. "Is that him? I'll kill him." Big Buns launched himself through the door, knocking it off its hinges, because that was the fastest way out into the waiting room. The secretary tried to say something about witnesses, but Big Buns was on the frail Oriental before she could speak. The old man could scarcely have weighed ninety pounds, and he was old. The secretary

53

closed her eyes, waiting for the crunch.

There was no crunch. There was a bang. Big Buns had landed on the chair. Now he was on the floor, and the little old man was standing calm.

"Fool," said the Oriental, "why do you give away such violence? I wish to purchase it from you."

Big Buns wanted to crush the old man like dried pretzels. He didn't know why he had missed him on his first lunge, but he was sure his second one would make the gook into crumbs.

Then again, Tituccio was listening through the broken door. And the old man had said giving away free violence was stupid, and Tituccio would think so, too, especially after Big Buns got stuck with that raw wood desk.

"Five thousand dollars," said Big Buns Bonafante.

"A very smart price. An honorable price," said the Oriental, who insisted they talk in private, which was hard because the door that made things private was now in splinters.

So everyone had to leave the office, but for $5,000, everyone thought that was a smart thing to do, so it was all right.

The Oriental told Big Buns that he was in search of

someone to teach a lesson—not to kill but to teach someone else that he was not invincible.

"How'd you find me?" Big Buns asked.

"To get a certain level of person, one must go to the waterfronts of the world. You are, of course, in no great way skilled, but having gotten paid for violence, you should have a crude experience that will suffice."

"Whaddya mean, crude?"

"When you are done, I will explain," said Chiun.

"I gotta have the money up front."

And like an old fool, the Oriental gave him all the money. In gold, no less, five thousand dollars in a few ounces of gold.

Big Buns would show how smart he was by not doing anything for the money. As the old geezer dropped the heavy gold coins into his right hand, Bonafante felt a tingling in his wrist where the old man's long fingernails had touched them.

"Perhaps you think you will have to do nothing for your money," said the old man. "But your hands will not be your own if you should prefer being a thief to an assassin. See if that is still your hand. Take your gold if you can."

Big Buns tried to close his hand on the gold. but it didn't close. It felt as if it closed, but it stayed open, the fingers like stone, frozen there, not his own anymore.

The old man touched the wrist once more. "If you fail, I will do this to your whole body," he said. "You will lie on the ground, unable to move, until your body rots."

"Okay. But tell me one thing. How'd you know I was gonna walk with the money?"

"Very simple," said the Oriental. "When one recruits at the waterfront, one gets thieves as well as murderers."

And so the deal was struck. Big Buns was to see the Oriental walking along a street in Rye, New York. Big Buns and two others with clubs were to attack the white man Chiun was with and then retreat after breaking no more than two bones. All that was needed was to show the white man that he was not invincible. Big Buns had one last question. Why, if the Oriental could make Big Buns helpless, did he not do the work himself?

"Because my pupil knows the Master cannot be beaten, but he does not know the world itself cannot be beaten. He has too much spunk for his own good."

And so on the appointed day, Big Buns and two men he had hired for fifty dollars each drove into Rye with lead pipes in their laps and waited on the street.

"No killing," said Big Buns. "We break a couple of bones and we go home."

"The guy must be big if you need help, Big Buns," said one of the day hires.

"Real big," said the other.

"Yeah," said Big Buns. "I guess so." But when they saw who was walking with the old gook, they all laughed. He was reasonably tall, but he was thin, except for thick wrists. He didn't look as if he would be any trouble, so Big Buns thought he would show off and do the job himself.

He got out of the car and yelled out, "You? What's your name?"

"Remo," said the man with the gook.

"You owe me a hundred dollars, and I want it now."

"Sure," said Remo. "I'd rather give you a hundred than kill you. I've got all sorts of money now." Remo gave the thug a hundred-dollar bill. He had picked up thirty of them in the morning. Unlimited funds were part of the job.

"I want another hundred interest," said Big Buns, and the skinny guy with the gook gave him another hundred and kept walking.

"Hey, you. I don't like your face," Big Buns yelled.

"Okay," said Remo gently. He was busy asking Chiun a question about breathing and didn't want to be bothered with someone trying to pick a fight.

Big Buns gaped as the Oriental who had hired him and the man he was supposed to break walked on down the street. Big Buns followed and ran in front of Remo.

"Get off my sidewalk," said Big Buns. At this point, Remo would have to stop the conversation to step into the gutter.

So, as he was taught and without breaking stride, Remo allowed his right hand to move through the throat of the hulk in his way. He did this with proper breathing. He did this totally centered on himself, a simple stroke, very basic and very clean.

And he said to Chiun, "That's what I meant by the breathing. The stroke comes out of it, right? I mean, the breathing doesn't come from the stroke, but the stroke comes from the breathing."

Big Buns lay on the street, skin and hairline where a neck had been. His face was pressed against the cement sidewalk, his barrel chest straight to the blue sky. His body twitched once and was still forever.

Remo showed his hand to Chiun. "See. No marks, no blood. Nothing. Perfect."

"Hmmmmm," said Chiun.

"You don't seem happy," Remo said. "It wasn't a difficult stroke, but it was executed properly. You always said you preferred the modest, simple stroke to the complex."

And if that wasn't bad enough, Chiun saw the oafs Bonafante had hired. They came trundling out of a car, wielding lead pipes above their heads, their entire bodies open to any blow, their weight driving forward, making them plump geese on a platter. They couldn't stop themselves. And of course in this situation, Remo had to show off: inner moves, outer moves, ups, double ups and a concentrated inside-out shoulder thrust, dropping them with the grace of flower petals. Remo waited for his compliment.

"You should have kept it simple."

"When you have Sinanju like I have, maybe you don't have to," Remo said.

"You don't have Sinanju," Chiun said.

"It ain't chop-saki."

And he was right. He had learned too much too soon. And he was continuing to learn on his own. When Chiun was gone, Remo would tell the world he had Sinanju, and who would be there to show he didn't?

A better level of assassin would have to be hired to teach the lesson.

CHAPTER
FIVE

BEASLEY DALWORTH PROFESSED to the gracious crowd at the Dunnington Country Club in Dunnington, Connecticut, that he really didn't know what to do with another trophy except "love it. And love you. Brad here played fine golf. And win or lose, a round with Brad is always a win."

Beasley smiled his perfect smile. He was in his early fifties, and his immaculately groomed hair had grayed with such grace around the temples that it looked as if an advertising artist had painted it in to encourage people to want to grow old.

Everyone in Dunnington said Beasley should have been a male model. That is, when they weren't saying that Beasley should have gone on the pro golf tour because Beasley always shot around par—except under pressure, when he would shoot the eyes out of par.

Beasley had just won the club championship for the seventh time in a row, defeating a young man named Brad so badly that the match was over halfway through.

Beasley also played top-grade tennis, and it was said that he had the kind of game that could have gone on the tennis circuit when he was younger.

The old money in Dunnington knew he wasn't quite old money, but he wasn't nouveau riche either. He was something special, a very attractive man who, in a society that kept its emotional distance, was just farther away than anyone else.

He used the word "love" a lot, but no one had even gotten close enough to him to feel friendly. In a town where most conversation was mindless small talk about the weather, grass, and martinis, Beasley Dalworth's talk was the smallest of all. He could say hello with less meaning than a doorman.

Every so often, Beasley would disappear. Sometimes once a year, twice a year, or maybe for a full year at a time. Beasley, everyone said, had some sort of international trade arrangement, but no one ever got close enough to Beasley to find out what.

A delivery boy, it was said, had seen guns in Beasley's house, not displayed on a wall like a hunter's, but stacked under a tarpaulin. A retired army officer said Beasley's house was really a disguised bunker, with lawns as potential fields of fire.

This day, as Beasley Dalworth received his seventh trophy, an Oriental in a saffron robe stood at the edge of the crowd. Orientals were not allowed as members of the Dunnington Country Club, so everyone assumed he was a cook. Yet this "cook" made the Dunnington members somehow feel looked down upon. They were supposed to be excluding him, but somehow everyone who came near this old man felt that they were the ones being excluded.

Annoyed, they kept saying "Excuse me, excuse me," to let him know he was in the way, but he would not answer. Finally, someone said, "Excuse me. Why don't you answer?"

"Because you're not excused," said Chiun. And they weren't. He wanted to speak to Dalworth.

"I am afraid, sir, he is busy."

"No, he is not. He is just finishing a silly little white man's game. And you're the wrong whites to be playing it anyway," said Chiun. "You're not Scots."

"I am sorry, sir, but you are going to have to leave. You are not a member, and I don't know whose guest you are."

"His," said Chiun, pointing to Beasley Dalworth. "I am his guest."

62

"Does he know that?"

"He will when I tell him."

The stunned member watched the Oriental ease through the crowd and take the cup away from Dalworth.

"Come. We play a real game," Chiun said.

"I beg your pardon," said Dalworth."

"You don't have it," said Chiun. "I have been watching your little attempts to do business and have allowed them to go on. In Vienna, in Kowloon, in Sidney, in Bucharest. Dalworth, give me clubs and we will play."

"You're not from…" Dalworth could not get out the words. The club members watched as he actually flushed, then said, "Are you from a village on the West Korea Bay?"

"Of course," said Chiun.

"Yes. Well, let us play," said Dalworth. He turned to the crowd and said, "It's all right. He is an old friend and my guest. And I want to play another round."

Clubs were brought for the strange guest. Who did not like the balls. He wanted gutta-percha balls.

"Sir, those kind of balls haven't been used in a half-century," said one club member.

"Too bad," said Chiun. "They were good balls."

Everyone at the club would remember this day as long as

they lived because Beasley Dalworth, who had just shot a nine-under-par 63, teed up his ball, swung, and missed. He missed the ball entirely.

Then he swung again and missed again.

He missed five times until the Oriental put a long-nailed finger on his back, which seemed to calm the club champion. The flush left his face, his hands stopped shaking, and he hit the ball perfectly down the fairway 275 yards.

That was more like it, like the Beasley everyone knew.

The Oriental kept handing back clubs. He didn't like the driver. He didn't like the irons or any of the woods. Finally he took an old blade putter from someone's bag.

He did not tee up the ball. Instead, he looked at the green 420 yards away and muttered, "No."

"No, what?" asked a club member.

"It does not break left to the hole."

"That's a four-hundred-yard putt, sir,"

Chiun shrugged. "A ball must land somewhere. Why not where it is supposed to?"

And then the putter came back. Every golfer worked on a slow backswing, but people would later remember that this backswing seemed languidly slow, as if the club would fall asleep in the hands of the slight Oriental. They would

64

remember that most thought it was only a practice jiggle because the club just seemed to return to the ball as slowly as it had left.

A banker, though, who had played golf all his life, would tell others that for the first time, he actually saw with his own eyes a golf ball compress. He said the putter just touched the ball and it flattened out.

The ball started out high and kept going, impervious to the winds like a small aspirin hurled into orbit. Some lost sight of the ball against the white clouds.

But they all saw it land, bang onto the green, and then start rolling toward the cup. It rolled around the edge of the cup and then stopped six inches away.

"Wow," gasped the crowd. Several applauded and one woman cheered. And a man cracked a joke about this magnificent shot, the finest golf shot they had ever seen anywhere.

"But it didn't go in," the man joked. "You missed."

"What do you expect if you have weak rims on your cup? You do better," Chiun said.

"I was joking."

"You have awful greens. No one should play this game but a Scot."

65

"We were joking. That is the best golf shot we've ever seen."

"And really good golf courses are by the ocean and should have some salt in the air. This course is inland," said Chiun.

"We're saying it's a great, fantastic shot."

"And your teeing area isn't level," said Chiun and then, realizing that everyone would follow them and they would not be alone, Chiun told Dalworth he would speak with him in private, which turned out to be Dalworth's home.

When the doors were shut and windows activated to detect any bugging devices that might have been planted, Dalworth said, with tremors in his voice, "You are Sinanju."

"You have said it," said Chiun.

"I've heard. Some of my best clients would mention that their ancestors would hire Sinanju and that while I might be good, Sinanju was beyond that. Way beyond that. But I thought the House of Sinanju had died out."

"Do you not believe your eyes, white man?"

"I believe. Everywhere I have gone, I have heard of the legends of Sinanju. What are you doing in America, and what do you want of me?"

"I want you to injure someone," said Chiun.

"But, Master, you certainly don't need someone as

66

unworthy as me."

"White, I like your attitude. But yes, I do need you. I cannot be the one to injure this person because he knows I am Sinanju. But if he sees someone else injure him, he will know he can never become Sinanju."

"You want me to go to your village?" Dalworth said.

"He is not in the village. He is in this country."

"You have trained someone in America?"

"Yes," Chiun said.

"But why would you come here, if I might ask, to train a Korean?"

"He is not Korean," said Chiun, lowering his eyes briefly. How this white could ferret out shame.

"You have trained a white in Sinanju?" said Dalworth.

He offered Chiun libations, tea or rosewater or jasmine essence. The Master of Sinanju refused.

"Yes," said Chiun. "I have trained a white."

"Then train me. I will do your bidding. I know of Sinanju and I appreciate, in my meager way. I have studied the art of the assassin, O Master. Train me."

"No," said Chiun. "It was an accident that I trained this white. And that is what I wish to end."

"Command and I obey."

"I wish that you injure him."

"With a weapon?" asked Dalworth.

"If you wish. But just injure. Do not kill."

"A crippling injury?"

"No. He must have all his abilities when this is done. A bone. Bones break and bones knit."

"It is important to you that he not be permanently injured?"

"I have said it," Chiun intoned.

"If I had but one ray of the power of Sinanju, the sun source of all the killing arts, I would not need a weapon. All my life, in all my training, I have wondered about Sinanju. Every time I picked up a weapon, I knew it was a lesser weapon because it was not Sinanju but a manufactured weapon. All my skills are but nothing in thy awesome light."

"Beasley Dalworth, if all whites were like you, there would be no problems on this earth," said Chiun.

"Teach me Sinanju, Master. I will give you all I have."

"Would that I could, O decent white. But I live by my traditions and I cannot."

"But you have taught a white, O Master, O Light unto us barbarians. Teach me; I will carry your traditions with respect."

"No," said Chiun. "Done is done and the universe has its

laws. We of Sinanju, over the centuries, never made a law but followed them better than others. We learned them. We learned our bodies and the powers that are. And they say done is done. What price do you ask for your service?"

"But to serve you," Dalworth said.

"Do not be an amateur with me at this moment, Beasley Dalworth, worthy white."

"Then two ingots of gold that I might honor them for the rest of my life."

"Done," said Chiun.

Dalworth heard the instructions. Never before had he allowed anyone to tell him how to perform a service. He had worked for intelligence agencies on both sides of the Iron Curtain, and he knew that if they could have improved his methods one iota, they would not have come to him for service. But now he listened. He heard his first delicious tidbit about Sinanju.

Watching the long fingernails trace firing patterns, he began to understand Sinanju. It was in the way of life itself. Because here was this man who never used a gun, showing all the right approaches for a gun ambush and why they would not work on this man called Remo.

"You see, as he breathes he is really part of all that is

around him, and if you set up here," said Chiun, "he will sense it." And then, pointing to Dalworth's second spot, he said, "Or here. He will sense that, too. But if you come here, moving slowly, along this line, he will not even know you are there, but rather think of you as just some passerby."

Beasley was smiling. "How did you know I would have taken those angles, Master?"

"Because they are the best, but they are thousands of years old. They are as old as a jungle trail."

Dalworth bowed and promised to be at the appointed place moving in the prescribed direction. But even as he bowed, he knew he must have Sinanju.

He would do everything he was told, except one thing. He would not shoot an arm. He would put the bullet in the center of the heart.

For this Oriental had brought Beasley Dalworth the one last thing he wanted and never thought he could have. Sinanju.

For if the Master of Sinanju had taught one white, he would teach another.

After his first white was killed.

CHAPTER SIX

"'I DON'T FEEL LIKE A WALK," REMO SAID.

"That is why you need one," Chiun said.

"The last time you wanted me to take a walk, three guys jumped me."

"Does that mean you will never walk again?" said Chiun.

"I don't feel like a walk."

"It is good for you. Do it."

"Why?" Remo asked.

"Because I am the Master of Sinanju. All you do is ask me questions. There are others in this world who would give all to be taught Sinanju, and all you do is question it."

"I thought you were leaving. Go teach them. Why are you hanging around here?"

"I am leaving. And when I am gone, how you will miss me," Chiun said.

"Yeah, I'll miss you," said Remo, getting dressed in what had now become his normal clothes. A black T-shirt, soft leather loafers so that his feet could move properly within them instead of being tied tight, and a pair of chinos.

"Ah, you will miss the glory of Sinanju?" Chiun said.

"No. Screw the glory. I kind of like you, you know."

"Of course you like me. I am Chiun."

"No, I don't think most people deeply like you," Remo said.

"They adore me."

"I don't know anyone who does."

"You have a vicious mouth. And you're a liar," Chiun said.

"It's hard to know," said Remo, and the words "Little Father" almost came out of his mouth. Which was strange because he had never had a father that he knew. "It's hard to know you, Chiun," Remo finally said.

"It's not hard. The world is just stupid."

"I like you. Everything I ever had in my life was taken away from me. I never had relatives. I never really had a home. I belonged, you know, to the Marines…now this outfit. I went to a high school and we won a football trophy, and they

72

said nobody would ever forget us. But we won so many trophies, they started throwing them away. And the coach I had who said I was the best middle guard he ever had…he didn't even remember my name. I never had anyone."

"Well, you do not have me, either," Chiun said. "I am leaving."

"I know. I was just telling you how I feel."

"You want to be an assassin? Get used to being lonely and unappreciated."

"I never said I wanted to be an assassin. I'm in this thing because, well, because I'm in it. And I believe in my country."

"Yes, of course. Your country. Not Sinanju. You never believed in what you were given. You never appreciated what I offered."

"What do you want from me?" said Remo.

"Don't say you like me, and let us go for our walk."

"Well, I do like you."

"Why?" asked Chiun.

"I eat orange peels, too, sometimes. I'm funny. I was the only guy in the Marines who liked basic training."

"You are a beast," Chiun said, and they left for their walk, with Chiun reminding Remo that he was already packed and anxious to leave this land that did not appreciate him and wanted him to continue throwing pearls before swine.

On a side street in downtown Rye, New York, Remo thought he saw a man walking toward him to shake hands. He thought he saw something. He thought he saw a flash from a man who was walking toward him to shake hands. A man with graying hair at the temples. But he wasn't shaking hands. He was creating the flash. And Remo's expanded perception noticed something. He noticed the flash touched him, and even as it touched him, he started to move away, to release the path of what he saw.

He had done this in training with Chiun. But in training he had always been away before the missile came. Now it was here.

It was in him, undeflected, going to the heart, hurling him back with its velocity as his internal organs caught the full force of the lead slug.

There was no air in his lungs, no power in his arms. He felt the hot blood beat out of him with the last spasms of his heart.

He was on his back, and Chiun was above him. Chiun had been right. Remo did not have Sinanju. He could not have been surprised so easily if he had really been in the process of becoming Sinanju.

He was going to die. He wanted to tell Chiun that he was

sorry, sorry for thinking he was Sinanju, sorry for being so presumptuous, sorry because now he was paying that last price.

He saw the old man's weathered face, and he saw that Chiun understood. They did not have to talk. Done was done and the universe was the universe. It went on as it had always gone on, without beginning and without end.

And Remo was now a part of it in darkness.

Chiun saw the life go. There was the body, warm, and the heart reflex still beating. But the life was not there.

In that instant, Chiun knew. Remo was gone.

But he was gone in such a peaceful way, in a way so unified with the universe that Chiun remembered his own training at the most advanced level.

This had come out of Remo, so naturally, so infinitely accepting.

Chiun stepped back from the body. The spine was aligned. Remo had centered himself even in death. The hands were drawn in as taught. The legs closed as had been taught. All the lessons properly learned, now in death done.

There, as clear as a great solar explosion, was the essence of the man, performing. Remo had taken Sinanju. He had taken it into his being. That was why he had learned so well. His essence had taught him.

This white man had been aligned with the universe. As only the Great Wang had been before, this man had been.

The essence was still there. And Chiun implored it, even as his long fingernails plunged into the chest. Bodies could repair themselves. That was what made the body survive. Lungs could breathe again, if there was life.

"The long night is not for you," screamed Chiun. "You are one. You are total with Sinanju. Come back. We do not reject you. We welcome you, my son. Come back."

The hands worked the heart that had stopped. The nervous system would have to take over from the damaged organs and could if they had been properly enhanced. How much they had been enhanced Chiun would find out now.

He worked one hand on the heart and the other along the spine. Greater medicine knew no men than the Masters of Sinanju, for all of them had been taught that killing was so small a part, the great part being life.

Chiun found the response. It was working. The white man's hands clenched, showing that the muscles still lived. The brain, so limited, according to Sinanju teaching, to one part in ten, now used two parts in ten, then three.

The lungs heaved. Spittle formed on the lips. A low, moaning birth sound of the earth came tipping from the throat.

Pitiful baby kicks went out from the knees. The fingernails, the very extremities, turned blue and then pink and then burning red. Blood came vomiting out of the mouth.

The spine twitched, and Chiun felt the heart, strong in his hands, pumping against his palm. It needed no massage. Remo had come back to help him, back to help the body live.

"My son, my son, I was wrong," wept Chiun to the beautiful child who had gone to death so well-trained and had come back at his father's call.

"My son, my perfect son."

"What?" said Remo. The voice was his again. And then Chiun realized that now Remo would remember everything he heard.

"You almost lost your life, idiot. Don't you remember anything I teach? Anything?"

"Why are you crying, Little Father?" asked Remo in the words he would use ever thereafter.

"I am not crying. I am so embarrassed by your incompetence that I am furious. I cannot leave now. You are too inept even to walk the streets."

"Okay," said Remo weakly.

"Not that I ever expect you to appreciate what I do for you," Chiun said.

"Okay," said Remo. There was a great tiredness in him, and the wound began to pain as the numbness went. But Chiun had taught him to deal with pain. He knew pain.

And he could have sworn that he had gone and dreamed of a great death. And that two voices had called him back.

• • •

In the darkness of a starless midnight, Chiun walked across the rolling lawn of Folcroft Sanitarium to sit under a birch tree. He wore the long, flowing black funeral robe, a robe given to him by his father. Just as his father had been laid to rest in an identical black robe given to him by his Master.

Chiun had no such robe to leave his successor, for he had no successor.

He had committed the unpardonable sin. He had broken faith with his ancestors, with the unbroken line of thousands of years, Master after Master, each of them continuing the honored traditions of the House of Sinanju. And now those traditions had been shattered, by Chiun himself, and he slowly sat down beneath the birch tree and waited for death to come to him.

Because death alone was what he deserved. At first, as he sat, the air was filled with the night sounds of the grassy wood.

78

Crickets chirped and birds whirred overhead. Bats sent noiseless signals whistling through the air. But soon there were no sounds as Chiun sank deeper and deeper into the silence of his own mind. For a moment, he wondered how death would come. Would it come quietly to claim its prize? Or would it sneer and mock and laugh at the one who had disgraced Sinanju?

"Come, death," he muttered. "But come as a friend. We have always been friends, you and I."

And then he heard a voice, but it was not the voice of death. It was a rich, full voice and it said, "Why do you sit there in the funeral robe, young Chiun?"

"Who is it?" Chiun asked. "Who speaks to me and calls me young?"

"Do you not know who I am?"

"No," Chiun said, for he did not know.

"Do you forget so easily that you were consecrated to me at birth?" the voice said.

"No," Chiun cried. "No, I cannot bear your being with me in my hour of shame."

"What shame?" the voice asked.

"I violated the legend," Chiun said. "First I trained one who was not dead. And then when I thought to punish him

79

for learning too much, I could not do that. I could not let him die. I am the most worthless of Masters."

The voice laughed. It came from everywhere and nowhere, but its echo reverberated inside Chiun's head.

"You did not violate the legend," the voice said. "You fulfilled it. For he was not dead, but you made him dead. And now he will be the dead night tiger made whole by the Master of Sinanju. He will be the greatest Master of all. For he is created Shiva, the Destroyer; Death, the Shatterer of Worlds."

"But he is white," Chiun said. "I have given Sinanju to an outsider."

"And if he stands in the sun for a year of summers, will he then still be white?" the voice asked.

"I do not understand," Chiun said.

"His skin is his skin and it is only his skin," the voice said. "But his heart is ours. His heart is Korean. His heart is Sinanju."

There was a pause and then the voice intoned, "Rise, Chiun. Stand."

Slowly, his eyes still closed. Chiun moved to his feet.

"Hear you now this. That from this day on, Chiun, Reigning Master of Sinanju, will make of this white night tiger a Master unlike all Masters who have gone before. He will be the greatest Master of all of us, young Chiun. And when you have come finally, when your teaching is done, to join us, we will all rise to greet you, as the greatest of teachers because yours was the greatest pupil of all. Henceforth, child, you will be known as Chiun the Teacher. And we will all honor you."

The voice sounded so close, Chiun could feel the breath of air on the back of his neck. But when he opened his eyes and turned, none was there.

The crickets again chirped and the birds whirred overhead and the bat signals whistled through the night. And Chiun lifted his face toward heaven and he said, "O Great Master Wang. I have heard your words, and this unworthiest of Masters waits for the day he may join you and bask in your reflected glory. But until that day, I will obey. I will be Chiun the Teacher."

• • •

At Folcroft's infirmary, the surgeon who repaired the wounds called it "one for the books." He had never seen anyone come back from such body damage.

"It just goes to show you that the body is a mystery," he said. "It's got powers to recover we don't even suspect."

Chiun waited until Remo was eating properly and then,

when Remo became suitably insulting and ungrateful, he realized his pupil was recovering fully and Chiun left him.

"Where are you going, Little Father?" Remo asked.

"I must be about our business."

• • •

Beasley Dalworth said he was glad to see the Master of Sinanju. He said he hoped his services had been adequate.

Chiun nodded.

"I might have jerked the gun at the last moment," Dalworth said. "I was so enamored of your fluid movements, O Master."

"You did not jerk the gun," Chiun said.

"Well, then, what brings you here?" said Beasley, who thought that now the other pupil was dead, he would be taught Sinanju. "I have come to bring you a gift," Chiun said.

"But why?"

"Because you killed my pupil, but in killing him, you taught me he was truly my son. He was of Sinanju. How this can be for a white thing, I do not know. But he is worthy of Sinanju."

"But he is dead," Dalworth said.

Chiun shook his head. "He was dead. But now he lives. He lives on, ever, as Shiva, the Destroyer. To live as that, first he had to die. As you were the instrument of that death, you in truth have raised him to glory. That is why I bring you a gift."

"And what is that gift, O Master?"

"A sudden ending without pain and without shame."

Dalworth's body was found a week later when the stench finally wafted into downtown Dunnington. His face had been sheared off, by a power no less than that of a hydraulic machine.

For months afterwards, the citizens of Dunnington locked their doors to keep out what the newspapers called "the hydraulic monster."

But the monster never struck again.

Back in Folcroft, Chiun supervised the recovery. Remo's love of his country would have to be worked on. It seemed stubbornly resistant to logic and the light of Chiun's wisdom. Also, Remo would have to produce an heir with a suitable Korean woman. Chiun would take care of that.

Remo would also have to learn by heart the history of the Masters and their contributions to Sinanju.

Chiun, of course, would have to be remembered as the one who took a white and taught him Sinanju because of Chiun's great glory, but it must be pointed out to all future Masters that Chiun did not do this by choice. And only one so great as Chiun should ever attempt anything so difficult.

Chiun was sure he would be called, after another thousand years or so, Chiun the Great Teacher. Or maybe Chiun the Greatest Teacher. But for now, he would settle for Chiun the Teacher. That would be Remo's responsibility, properly recording the greatness of his Master.

And of course they would have to move to Sinanju.

Unfortunately, this new future Master failed to see the true glory of Sinanju immediately.

"No, Little Father. I don't want to go to Sinanju. It's in Korea. That means it's cold and smells of human shit," said Remo,

"And you?" said Chiun. "You expect me to be able to teach such a pale piece of pig's ear? After you said that? After you said that?"

"All right. What does it smell like, then?" asked Remo.

"When one gazes upon the sun, does one notice smell?" asked Chiun.

"If he's standing on a shit heap like Korea, he does," Remo said.

"I suppose," said Chiun, "that I deserve this abuse for trying to teach a white. I will not speak to you until you apologize."

84

"Sounds good to me," Remo said. "But one thing, Little Father."

"I am ignoring you."

"Go ahead. Ignore. But listen," Remo said. "When I was shot, I heard a voice."

"If it said anything nice, it wasn't my voice," Chiun said. "Delirium. That is all it was."

"No, Little Father," Remo said thoughtfully. "This wasn't your voice. It was a voice I never heard before."

"What did it say?"

"It said…it said…I'm not sure I remember. I think it said, 'I am created Shiva, the Destroyer; Death, the Shatterer of Worlds.' That was it. What does that mean, Little Father? Whose voice was that?"

"It was your voice, my son," Chiun said softly.

"What did it mean?"

"Perhaps one day I will tell you," Chiun said.

"Don't do me any favors."

"Count on it. I won't."

THE END

About the Authors

WARREN MURPHY was born in Jersey City, where he worked in journalism and politics until launching the Destroyer series with Richard Sapir in 1971. A screenwriter (*Lethal Weapon II*, *The Eiger Sanction*) as well as a novelist, Murphy's work has won a dozen national awards, including multiple Edgars and Shamuses. He has lectured at many colleges and universities, and is currently offering writing lessons at his website, **WarrenMurphy.com**. A Korean War veteran, some of Murphy's hobbies include golf, mathematics, opera, and investing. He has served on the board of the Mystery Writers of America, and has been a member of the Screenwriters Guild, the Private Eye Writers of America, the International Association of Crime Writers, and the American Crime Writers League. He has five children: Deirdre, Megan, Brian, Ardath, and Devin.

RICHARD BEN SAPIR was a New York native who worked as an editor and in public relations before creating *The Destroyer* series with Warren Murphy. Before his untimely death in 1987, Sapir had also penned a number of thriller and historical mainstream novels, best known of which were *The Far Arena*, *Quest* and *The Body*, the last of which was made into a film. The book review section of the New York Times called him "a brilliant professional."

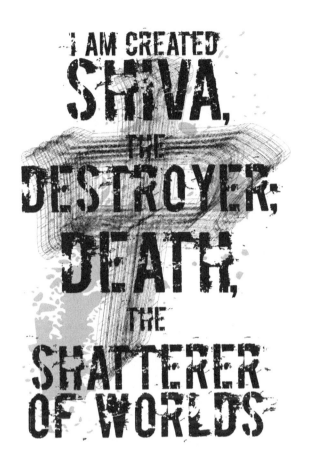
I AM CREATED SHIVA, THE DESTROYER, DEATH, THE SHATTERER OF WORLDS

© Devin Murphy, 2014

For more information on the *Destroyer* series, or just to say hello, please visit us at **DestroyerBooks.com** or **Facebook.com/DestroyerBooks**! Sign up for our mailing list for news, information, and free stuff!

Made in the USA
Middletown, DE
10 April 2020